Author's Dedication: To Grace Dunbar of Traralgon who spent a lifetime caring for wombats
Illustrator's Dedication: To Dr Peg and Wombles

Omnibus Books,
52 Fullarton Road, Norwood, South Australia 5067,
part of the ASHTON SCHOLASTIC GROUP
Sydney · Auckland · New York · Toronto · London

First published 1985
Reprinted 1985, 1986
First published in paperback (Omnibus/Puffin) 1989
Reprinted by Omnibus Books 1991, 1993

Text copyright © Thelma Catterwell 1985
Illustrations copyright © Kerry Argent 1985

Typeset by Caxtons Pty Ltd, Adelaide
Printed in Hong Kong

National Library of Australia Cataloguing-in-Publication entry
Catterwell, Thelma, 1945–
Sebastian lives in a hat.
ISBN 1 86291 098 7.
1. Wombats—Juvenile fiction. I. Argent, Kerry, 1960–
II. Title.

A823.3

Sebastian
lives in a hat

Written by Thelma Catterwell

Illustrated by Kerry Argent

Omnibus Books

Sebastian lives in a hat.
It's a brown woollen hat.

Sebastian's a pink fuzzy wombat.

He won't always be
pink and fuzzy.

The hat won't always be
big enough for him.

Sebastian hasn't always lived in a hat.
He used to live in a warm dark place.
It was his mother's pouch.

Sebastian feels safe in his hat.
It is warm and round and soft,
just like his mother's pouch.

Sebastian's mother was killed by a car. But he lay safe in her pouch.

He was very frightened when we found him and very, very hungry.

We held him close to keep him warm,
but he was soon cold.
We quickly found him
a hot water bottle.

We also found his hat.

Sometimes Sebastian leaves his hat to search for food.

Sebastian can't walk properly yet.
He wobbles a lot
then flops on his tummy and crawls.

Soon we find him.
We put him back in his hat
and he has his bottle.

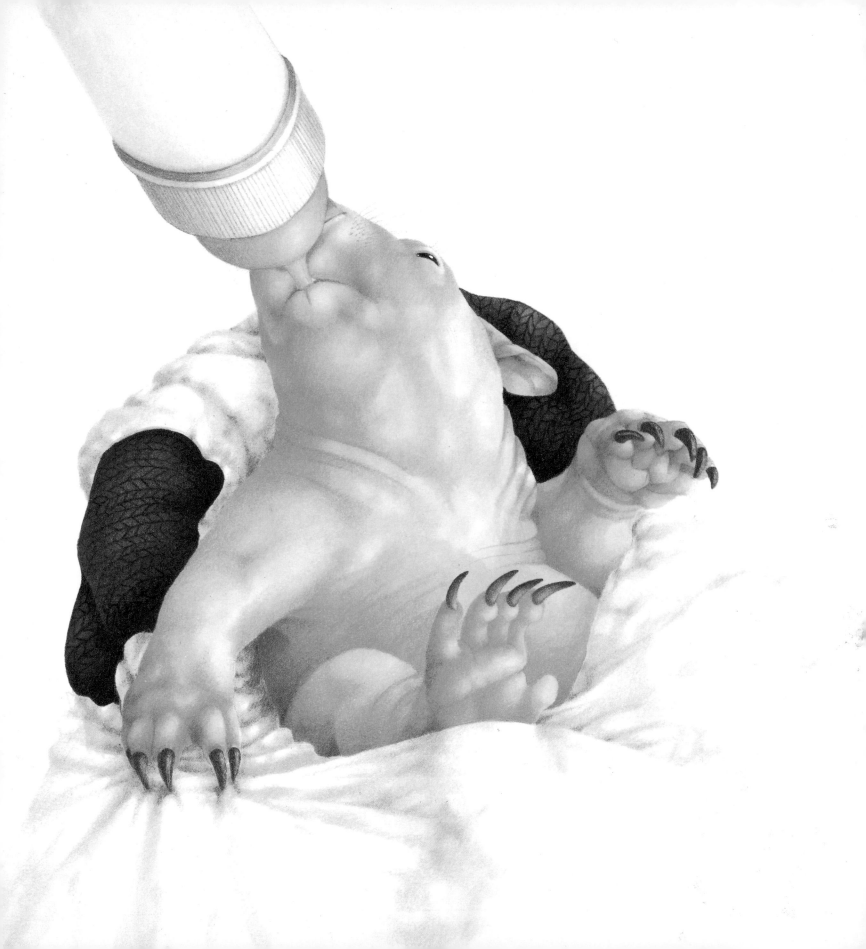

Sebastian's mother always kept
her pouch clean, so . . .
after his feed he has
a little job to do!

It was warm and damp in the pouch
and just right for Sebastian's skin.
We have to rub him with oil now
so his skin doesn't dry and peel.
Sometimes he enjoys that—
but not if our hands are cold.

Soon he goes back to sleep
in his warm woollen hat.

Sometimes Sebastian has to change his
brown hat for a grey hat.
We won't say why.
But when the brown hat is dry
Sebastian has it back again
and he is happy.

Every day Sebastian grows
a little bigger and stronger.
He has four sharp pointy teeth now
and sometimes he likes
to try them out.

He has strong sharp claws too
and one day he will use them
to dig a burrow for himself.

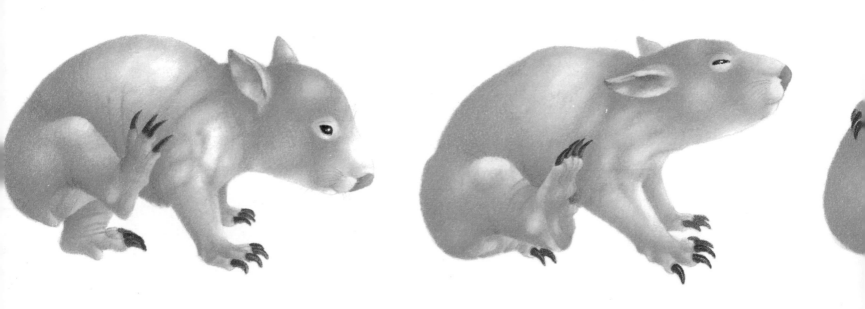

But right now they're just great
for having a scratch.

Sebastian's eyes are small and dark
and his ears are pink and big.
His nose is soft and spotty.

When he's big
his eyes and ears and nose
will help him find his way in the
bush at night.
And then he will do
what wombats should do . . .

But he may still love his hat.

What do you think?